The Homeless Christmas Tree

For information, please contact:
Brown Books Publishing Group
16200 North Dallas Parkway, Suite 170
Dallas, Texas 75248
www.brownbooks.com
972-381-0009
A New Era in Publishing™

ISBN: 1-933285-09-5
LCCN 2005930084
1 2 3 4 5 6 7 8 9 10

The Homeless Christmas Tree

Written by Leslie M. Gordon

Illustrated by Court Bailey

High atop a windswept Texas
hill stood a crooked little tree.
Nothing else was on the hill

—nothing at all.

From the hill,
the tree could see
a bustling highway.

Cars and trucks
rushed back and forth,
morning to night.

From the hill,
he could see a beautiful city.

At night,
the lights on the buildings
twinkled and glistened.

From the hill,
he saw lots of other trees.

But they were far away
and paid no attention to him.

"Of what use is one ugly little tree?"

This thought hurt his heart.
He was lonely

—and of no use at all.

*T*hen one Christmas Eve,
an old woman climbed the hill.

*S*he carried a sack.

*T*he sack was filled with
colored balls,
tinsel,
and garland.

She decorated the tree
with the lovely things.

He heard her say he was special.
"Special? Me? Really?"

*T*he woman said there were children in the city whose families had no homes.

*S*he knew this because at one time, she had been homeless.

*H*olidays were the hardest time of all for the children and their families.

*S*o she declared him the official Christmas tree for them.

The little tree
fairly burst with pride.

He stretched up tall
so the homeless people could
see him better.

*It continued this way for
many, many years.*

*On Christmas Eve,
the woman would come.*

*Together she and the tree
would conspire to bring
Christmas joy to the homeless.*

*T*hen one year, she didn't come.
The little tree was confused.

"*W*here is she?"

*P*eople in the city wondered also.

Although they didn't know it,
the little tree and his friend had
become celebrities.

The newspaper said
the old woman had become
too frail to climb the hill.

The tree drooped in despair.
There would be no Christmas tree
for the homeless!

Then something
wonderful happened.

People from the city
came to the hill with new
and different ornaments.

Up they climbed and before long,
beautiful decorations covered
every gnarled branch.

The little tree was happy for the
homeless—but sad at the same
time. He would never see his
dear friend again.

As the story of the little tree spread, the townspeople had an idea.

Why decorate just at Christmastime?

Homeless children might enjoy other holidays too.

So before Valentine's Day, they returned to the hill. Before long, red and pink hearts fluttered in the breeze.

At Easter,
more people came.

The misshapen little tree stood festooned with colorful pastel eggs.

Come September,
a special memorial was erected
on the hill next to the tree.

Three towering numerals
spelled out

9-11.

For Halloween,
the townsfolk hung
spiders,
bats,
and ghosts
from the tree's limbs.

It was kind of creepy,
but he remembered the children
and tried to be brave.

*T*hanksgiving
turkeys and pumpkins
were brought to the hill
in November.

*T*he little tree gave thanks
for all the wonderful people
who cared for others.

Finally, it was Christmas
and the people returned
with the tree's ornaments.

But that was not all they
brought. In the arms of a fireman
was the kind old woman.

She clutched
a gold star to her chest.

"This star and this tree are a
tribute to those less fortunate."

Her hand trembled
as she placed the star
at the very top of the
tree's crooked limbs.

The little tree stood
taller and straighter
than he had ever stood before.

And the light from his star
shone brightly

—for all the people in the city.